# Phoebe's Lost Treasure

By Barbara A. Roberts

Illustrated by Kate Sternberg

ADVANTAGE BOOKS

Published by Advantage Books
1001 Spring Street, #118
Silver Spring, MD 20910

Roberts, Barbara A., 1947–
    Phoebe's Lost Treasure / by Barbara A. Roberts; illustrations by
Kate Sternberg.
    p. cm. — (Phoebe Flower's adventures; 2)
    Summary: Trying to accomplish something special during the school
year, Phoebe Flower, a lively second grader, faces some difficulties but
ultimately succeeds with the help of her grandmother and her music teacher.
    ISBN  0-9660366-6-2
    [1. Self-esteem—Fiction.  2. Schools—Fiction.  3. Grandmothers—
Fiction.]    I. Sternberg, Kate, 1954–    ill.    II. Title.
III. Series: Roberts, Barbara A., 1947–    Phoebe Flower's adventures; 2.
PZ7.R5395P1        1999
[Fic]—dc21                                                    99-39427
                                                                    CIP
                                                                     AC

10  9  8  7  6  5  4  3  2 1
Printed in the U.S.A.

# Contents

"This book is dedicated to two very special women in my life.

Connie Roberts, my mother-in-law, who continues to show me through her unending generosity, devotion and spirit, that family is the true treasure of life

Katherine Sigel, my mother, who blessed me with a lifetime of laughter and love

I would also like to extend a special thanks to my family and friends who continue to support and encourage me."

B.R.

K.S.

# 1
# Dancing High

Being a heroine was great . . . for two days, anyway. The news of how I, Phoebe Flower, shimmied up the flag pole and rescued Jack, our class gerbil, spread throughout the school. Dr. Nicely, the school principal, stopped by my classroom and gave me a gold sticker that said, **"YOU ARE SPECIAL"** and shook my hand.

Ms. Biz, my teacher, said to me, "Phoebe, as a reward, you have my permission to take Jack home for the weekend."

When I got home, I was excited to set up Jack's cage. Buddy Dog sniffed around Jack and made strange growling noises. I think Buddy Dog was jealous of Jack.

Robbie, my best friend, cheered, "High five me, Phoebe. You're terrific!"

Walter, my two year old brother said, "Yea, Fee Fee," and clapped his hands whenever I came near him.

I even heard my sister, Amanda, who thinks she was born for one reason only . . . to be my boss, tell her friend on the phone, "You know, it was my sister who was the second grade heroine."

Mom couldn't stop smiling. She told me I had to call my dad who lives in New York City and tell him. Mom and Dad were divorced two years ago, but they still talk to each other.

I tried to make Mom think she was forcing me to call my dad. I really wanted to call him, but I said, "Oh no, I can't bother Daddy with this little teeny weeny bit of news."

"Little teeny weeny bit of news!" gasped

my mother. "Are you kidding? You are a heroine, Phoebe, and this is no little tiny bit of news." Amanda rolled her eyes to the ceiling.

When I finally got Dad on the phone, he thought I was wonderful too. "What a girl, I have! I am so proud of you. You are a brave little girl, Phoebe Flower," he shouted into the phone.

But my Grandma Wig was the happiest person of all when I told her my good news. Grandma Wig is my mother's mother and she lives three blocks from us. She got her name, Grandma Wig, from Amanda. Grandma's real name is Gert, but one day Grandma was coming to visit and Mom called Amanda and me together and said, "Girls, Grandma Gert is coming over to visit and she is wearing a wig. Don't say a word about it. Don't even look at her head. She thinks it looks just like real hair and we don't want her to think that we know it isn't. OK?"

"OK, Mom, not a word," we both promised.

When Grandma Gert walked in the door, Amanda and I both stared right at her head and then Amanda said, "Hi, Grandma Wig, you look very nice today."

My mom and my grandma burst out laughing. Amanda turned red in the face and my Grandma Gert has been Grandma Wig ever since. I think it's the only time that Amanda has ever made a mistake in her whole life.

I really think Grandma Wig likes me better than she likes Walter and Amanda. She almost never gets mad at me and when she comes over to our house she says, "Where is that sweetie, Phoebe?" Grandma Wig made me sit down and tell her the whole story about rescuing Jack. "Please, tell me one more time," she asked after I had already told her twice. I know for sure that I saw a little tear in her eye when she hugged me. "I am so proud of my little sweetie, Phoebe." Then, she said, "You know what I believe, Phoebe? That you'll never dance if you don't take a chance."

Well, after the rescue, I danced all right. For two days I danced. I danced to the bus stop. I danced off the bus. I danced down the halls in school, and I danced to my desk. I danced to lunch, and I danced to gym. Then, after those two very short days of being the heroine of the school, I danced to music class.

# 2
# Great Advice

My problem with music class began this summer when I had a heart-to-heart talk with Dad. A heart-to-heart talk is a talk that grown-ups want to have with you and they pretend that you want to have it too. I knew that my mom had told my dad that I didn't want to go to second grade. She had tried to get me to talk about my feelings, but I wouldn't say one word about school.

I remember the phone call. It was the hottest day of the summer. Robbie and I were sitting on my front step watching our popsicles drip into puddles and deciding whether to go swimming or just squirt each other with the hose.

"Phoebe!" Mom called me, "Come in the house. Your dad's on the phone. He wants to talk to you. Make sure you listen carefully to what he says."

My mother has never asked me to listen to anything my father said before. My brain was saying, "Phoebe , alert, alert, something's up!"

I sucked in the last mouthful of popsicle and walked into the kitchen with my head aching from the pain of the cold. "Hello, Dad," I said into the phone, trying to figure out what he was going to say that I had to listen to carefully.

From the first word of our conversation, I knew it was going to be a heart-to-heart. "Crazy as this may sound, Phoebe," started my dad, "I didn't always like school either. However, that changed for me when I realized one thing. Phoebe, are you listening to me?"

"Yes, I am, Dad," I answered, puffing short breaths into the phone. I had been twisting and turning as I talked on the phone, and had wrapped the phone cord around my whole body about eleven times.

"Are you okay, Phoebe? You sound out of breath," Dad asked with concern in his voice.

"Fine, Dad," I answered trying to sound fine. I knew I had better listen to my dad or he would tell me the same story over and over again and Mom would come and see if everything was all right and get mad at me for being tangled up.

"I totally agree with you, Father," I answered.

My dad started to tell me about his days at school when he was my age and how hard it was for him to pay attention to the teacher. "You have to be determined, Phoebe," my dad continued. "It's a big word that means that you have to keep on trying and believing that you can do anything you want to do. I mean that, Phoebe. I know you better than anyone else, except your mother, of course, and I know you can do anything if you try hard enough. You have to believe that, too."

I was so happy to be untangled from the

9

phone cord that I didn't realize my dad had stopped talking. After a minute of silence, I said, "Dad, are you still there?"

"Well, Phoebe?" Dad asked.

"I totally agree, Father," I answered again.

"Well . . . then, what is it that you agree to do? What are you going to be determined to do in second grade?" he asked me.

Yikes! My dad wanted an answer right then. I could feel myself start to twist the phone cord around my body again. "Let me have a minute to think about it, Dad. I want to be really sure," I answered .

So I thought and I thought for what seemed like two days. Then, I remembered how I wanted to be Gloria Von Kloppenstein in first grade when she sang all by herself in the first grade chorus at the end of the year. Yes! Yes! That's it!

"Dad, I know what I want to do. I want to sing a solo all by myself in the second grade chorus at the end of the year. I want to see the whole audience stand and clap and cheer. Dad, I want to sing. That's just what I will be determined to do," I answered.

"You want to sing a solo, Phoebe?" my dad

asked. "Can you sing?"

"Yep, that's it, Dad. Of course, I can sing. I think I can sing. No, of course, I can sing. Everybody can sing. Thanks for the advice. I feel like a brand new kid. I love you, Dad."

"Goodbye, Phoebe, I love you, too," Dad said quietly.

I untwisted the cord from my body like a ballerina and danced out to the front porch to tell Robbie I was ready to go swimming.

# 3
## Do-Re-Me

So, here I am dancing into music class and suddenly I remember what my dad and I talked about on the phone that hot summer day. I am Phoebe Flower, the school heroine. I am determined! I can do anything I want. I can sing. I can sing a solo all by myself in the second grade concert at the end of the year.

"Good afternoon, boys and girls!" says Miss Fasola.

"Good afternoon, Miss FASOLA!" we all answer.

"Remember, boys and girls, it's Miss Prissy FASOLA," she reminds us. "Now let's do that again."

"Good afternoon, Miss Prissy FASOLA," we all chant.

"Much, much better, class," she smiles.

Miss Prissy Fasola has black curly hair and black dirt under her eyes. When she smiles, she doesn't show her teeth. She doesn't smile a lot. She is in love with her name. She must be the only teacher in the whole wide world that tells kids her first name. I remember last year in first grade when Robbie told Mrs. Ward, our first grade teacher, that he heard his mother talking and he knew that her first name was Shirley. Mrs. Ward said, "My name is Mrs. Ward, and that's that, Robert!"

"Before we begin our class we will sing the scale," Miss Prissy Fasola says. "Remember, we sing softly until we get to my name and then we sing out loud in our best voices. Ready? Wait for the note that tells us to begin. One, two, three, go!"

We all start to sing softly, "do-re-me." Then the class gets louder on "FA-SO-LA" and then we quietly finish with "ti-do."

"Very nice, boys and girls, but someone was singing a little too loudly. Please, remember, a good voice does not have to be a loud voice," Miss Prissy Fasola grins.

Now that I know I can sing, I do agree with Miss Fasola. A good voice doesn't have to be a loud one. But if I am going to sing a solo all by myself in the second grade concert at the end of the year, I better let Miss Prissy Fasola know that I have a good voice. If I sing softly, she'll never hear me.

"Now, boys and girls," Miss Prissy Fasola claps her hands, "we will practice the song 'America the Beautiful.' It's one of my favorites. Ready, set, listen for the note to begin."

We all start to sing, "Oh beautiful for spacious skies." Miss Fasola smiles and waves her hands and nods her head.

I start to wonder how Miss Prissy Fasola is going to notice my good singing voice when everyone is singing together. I close my eyes

15

and I start to sing as beautifully as I can, "AMERICA, AMERICA, GOD SHED HIS GRACE ON THEE."

"Everybody STOP!" Miss Prissy Fasola yells and claps her hands. "Somebody is singing off key and way, way, too loud. Who is it?"

We all look around at each other. Nobody says anything. I begin to wonder who it is. I glance at Robbie who is sitting next to me. He starts blinking at me like he has dirt caught in both his eyes. Then he puts his pointer finger up to his lips like he wants me to be quiet. I think he's jealous of my voice.

"OK, let's start once again," Miss Fasola says. "One, two, three and remember, boys and girls, a good voice does not have to be a loud voice."

"Yes, that's true," I think to myself, "but, if she doesn't hear me, how will Miss Prissy Fasola know I have great voice, a great voice that should sing a solo in the second grade concert at the end of the year?"

"Oh beautiful, for spacious skies, for . . ." we all start to sing. Miss Prissy Fasola waves her left hand and smiles without showing her teeth. She starts to walk around the room.

"America, America," the class sings together.

"GOD SHED HIS GRACE ON THEE!" I let it blast out of my mouth.

"That's it, that's it! Stop everyone! I hear the voice now. It's over in that group in the corner of the room." Miss Fasola claps her hands and marches closer to the row where I am sitting.

I start to wonder who it is that's singing off the key. I do know that when Miss Prissy Fasola finds out who it is she'll be mad. She got mad at me once last year when I was in first grade and once was enough. I can see Robbie out of the corner of my eye. He has his hands around his neck like he is choking himself. He is acting so weird today. Maybe he wants me to laugh so I'll get in trouble. Sorry, not today, Robbie. Today, I'm going to be discovered.

"This will be the last time I say this, boys and girls. A good voice does not have to be a loud voice. Everyone will, once again, start from the beginning. I think we are all getting tired of starting from the beginning, aren't we? But, we will do this until we get it right, won't we, boys and girls?"

"Yes, Miss Prissy Fasola!" we all say at the same time.

"One, two, three, go!"

"Oh beautiful, for spacious skies," the class begins again.

Miss Fasola starts to walk back and forth, back and forth, and then, as she gets closer to where I am sitting, I know it's my chance to show off my great voice.

"GOD SHED HIS GRACE ON THEE!" I sing my best.

Miss Prissy Fasola gasps, "It's you, Phoebe Flower. It's you! You are screeching a song that is supposed to make you proud to be an American. You are singing off key and way, way, too loud. Three times today I told the class that a good voice does not have to be a loud voice. March to Dr. Nicely's office right now and I will meet you there after class."

Miss Fasola points to the door. She can't mean me. She's making a mistake. I don't just think I can sing. I know I can sing. I can do anything I want to. I am determined. My dad told me.

"But Miss Fasola," I beg, "how would you ever know I have a great voice if I don't sing loud so that you can hear me? How would you know to pick me to sing the solo all by myself in the second grade concert at the end of the year?"

"Out, Phoebe, out!" Miss Fasola points to the door.

# 4
# Another Bad Day

This is a mistake. I know it. My dad told me I could do anything I wanted to. I shuffled my feet to the office and muttered under my breath, "Miss Fasola thinks she's so la-di-da."

"Hi, Phoebe," Mrs. Walkerspeaking, the school secretary, greets me. "How's the little heroine doing and why the sad face, Phoebe? That's not a heroine's face."

"Hi, Mrs. Walkerspeaking," I say softly. "I'm having a bad day. Do you ever think you can do something and then find out you can't? Well, my dad said I can do anything I want if I am determined, and I am, but I still can't do it. Miss Fasola says I should be proud to be an American and that I ruined 'America the Beautiful.' She says I sing way, way, off the key. I have to see Dr. Nicely, and I can't sing anymore today because I am too loud. How will Miss Fasola know that I should be the one picked to sing the solo in the second grade concert at the end of the year if I don't sing loud enough for her to hear me? Do you know how to sing, Mrs. Walkerspeaking?"

"You have had a bad day, Phoebe," Mrs. Walkerspeaking says. "Yes, I love to sing. I remember my second grade end-of-the-year concert. Ricky Speck threw up all over my new dress and the smell made me feel sick to my stomach, so I sat down on the bleachers. My mother couldn't see me and thought I had fainted. She came running up to the bleachers screaming my name and trying to find me. The music teacher had to stop the concert and I had to leave the auditorium because I had throw-up all over me, and I smelled. There wasn't a drop of throw-up on Ricky Speck. All the kids were holding their noses, so they couldn't sing! The music teacher told me I ruined the whole concert."

"Really?" I say.

"Really!" answers Mrs. Walkerspeaking. "I'll let Dr. Nicely know that you're here, and don't worry, Phoebe, you have more talents than singing."

It seems like two days before Dr. Nicely opens her door. "Hi, Phoebe. Come on into my office. How are you today? Do you have a problem?"

"Well, Dr. Nicely, as a matter of fact, I do," I say as I get up and walk into her office. "You see, my dad and I had a heart-to-heart talk, and he says I can do anything if I am determined, and I am, but I can't. Miss Fasola says I ruined 'America the Beautiful' because I sing off the key. She says I make every one else ruin it too because I'm too loud. How will she ever know to pick me to sing the solo in the second grade concert at the end of the year if I don't sing loud enough for her to hear me? Did you know Mrs. Walkerspeaking ruined her second grade concert? Can you sing, Dr. Nicely?"

"Well, I guess I can, Phoebe, but there are a lot of other things I can't do," Dr. Nicely answered. "I can't whistle and I can't ice skate."

"Gee, that's too bad, Dr. Nicely," I tell her. "I am pretty good at both of those things."

"See, Phoebe, we all have special talents," Dr. Nicely smiles, "so please try to sing softer in music class. Miss Fasola is proud of the way her children sing and she believes that a good voice . . ."

". . . does not have to be a loud voice," we both say together and laugh.

"Well, I'll try, Dr. Nicely, but I did promise my dad," I answer.

"Please try, Phoebe, because we don't like to see Miss Fasola angry, do we?" Dr. Nicely asks. "Now, I'll have to write a note home to your mother and you'll have to apologize to Miss Fasola. Maybe you could think of some-thing else to be determined to do. I'm sure your father wouldn't care if you changed your mind."

"OK, I'll try," I say sadly to Dr. Nicely, "but, I really wanted to sing a solo in the second grade concert at the end of the year and hear

everyone cheer."

I start to open the door and Dr. Nicely calls, "Cheer up, Phoebe, and remember, a good voice . . ."

". . . doesn't have to be a loud voice," I finish and giggle.

I wish I could rip up this note. I'm sure my mom will find out if I do, and then I'll really be in trouble.

Later that night, while Mom's making dinner and holding Walter in one arm, I give her the note. Maybe, if I'm lucky, she'll put it down and forget to read it.

"Phoebe Flower!" my mother shouts at me from the kitchen. "Why did you get Miss Fasola so angry? You shouldn't be told three times not to sing so loud. Did you forget . . . Miss Fasola is our neighbor? I see her jogging when I walk Buddy Dog. I see her at the grocery store. What am I going to say to her the next time I see her?"

"It's Miss Prissy Fasola, Mom, Miss P. F." I tell her, "and I have an idea . . . maybe you should tell Miss Prissy Fasola that I want to sing a solo all by myself in the second grade concert at the end of the year. I want to see the whole audience stand and clap and cheer."

Amanda bursts out laughing. "Are you kidding?" she says during screams of laughter. "Who told you that you could sing, Phoebe? You are crazy!"

"Please, Amanda, be nice," sighs Mom. "Phoebe's not crazy. She's just a little unsure of herself."

"She sounds pretty sure of herself to me," Amanda answers. "Even I know Gloria Von Kloppenstein will be picked to sing the solo at the end of the year concert and I'm not even in second grade. Gloria sings like an opera singer! Phoebe, **you don't!**"

"Please, girls," Mom begs, "Grandma Wig is coming for dinner. Let's not tell her about this note and please don't argue in front of her."

"Great idea!" I answer.

"I'll try!" Amanda says with a mean smile.

# 5

## What Time Is It?

    I start to set the table. I can't wait for Grandma Wig to come. She always cheers me up. Sometimes she brings me a little present. But, even if she doesn't, I love her anyway.

    "Hi, Mama!" I hear Walter yell as the front door opens.

    "Hi, Punkie!" Grandma yells back to Walter.

    I run up to Grandma and throw my arms

around her waist. "Hi, my sweetie, Phoebe!" she says as she hugs me back. "Something smells very good in here and I'm pretty hungry."

"Dinner is almost ready!" Mom yells from the kitchen. "Phoebe, go upstairs and get Amanda, please."

"Hurry back, Phoebe, I can't wait to hear about your day at school," Grandma Wig says with a smile.

During dinner Grandma tells us about her day at the grocery store and how she saved $.75 on cat food. She tells us about her Bingo game at the senior citizen hall and how some of her friends are getting car phones. Then, the worst happens.

"So, Phoebe and Amanda, tell me about your day at school," Grandma Wig asks.

I look at my mom. She looks at me.

"Well, Grandma," Amanda starts, "I won my spelling bee today. I was the only one in my class that could spell the word encyclopedia. Then, because I am such a wonderful listener, my teacher picked me to take charge of the room while she went to find the custodian."

"Very good, Amanda, I am proud of you.

What a great day you had!" Grandma says. "Thank you, Grandma Wig," Amanda smiles. "Phoebe, it's your turn to tell Grandma about your day."

"Oh, it was OK. I've had better. I'm line leader this week, though," I say.

"You're only line leader because all the other girls in your class already had their turn, Phoebe. Tell Grandma what happened in music, why don't you?" Amanda smirked.

"Amanda, you promised," says Mom.

"Oops," smiles Amanda, "I guess I forgot."

"What happened, sweetie, Phoebe?" asks Grandma. "You can tell me. I love to hear all about your day, the good and the bad."

"Well, Grandma," I begin, "when I talked to my dad this summer, he told me I could do anything I wanted if I tried hard enough. He said that all I needed was determination and I would be happy. So I thought and I thought about what I wanted to do. I decided I wanted to sing a solo in the second grade concert at the end of the year just like Gloria Von Kloppenstein did in first grade. I want to see the whole audience stand and clap and cheer. But . . . Miss Prissy Fasola said I sing way off the key and too loud and that I ruined 'America the Beautiful.' How will she know I can sing if I don't sing loud? That's what I want to know. She sent me to the office, and she was mad. Mom says she sees Miss Prissy in the grocery store and now she'll be embarrassed to see her."

"You forgot the part about how she had already warned you three times," adds Amanda.

"Amanda, please!" sighs Mom.

"Listen, Phoebe," says Grandma Wig, "I always wanted to sing, too, but I never was very good. How about if you and I think of something else you can be determined to do? Your dad won't care, I'm sure. He just wants you to be happy. We'll think of something after dinner, OK?"

"Why don't you be determined to stay out of trouble for one whole day," Amanda laughs.

After dinner, Grandma sits on the couch and I plop down next to her. She puts her arm around me and we snuggle. "Can you tie your shoe, Phoebe?" she asks me.

"Yeah, I learned how to do that this summer," I tell her.

"Let's see, can you tell time?"

31

"Well, sort of, I guess. I can read the clock in Mom's bedroom."

"I mean, can you tell time on a real clock or a watch; the clocks that have hands that go around, like the clock in the kitchen?" Grandma asks.

"No, not yet," I tell her.

"Then, that's it, Phoebe. You can be determined to tell time by the end of the school year. That's something you'll feel proud of and so will your dad and mom. I'll be able to help you, and Miss Fasola won't be mad because you won't be singing too loud. What do you think?" Grandma asks again. "We can start tonight."

"Oh, OK," I admit. "Maybe singing wasn't such a great idea."

Grandma teaches me that the small hand tells the hour and the big hand tells the minute, which makes no sense to me. The big hand should tell the hour because it's bigger. She teaches me that when the big hand touches a number it is a five-minute number. Grandma tells me that if I can count by fives, I can figure out the time. I was happy that I could tell her I could count by fives.

# 6

# The Best Gift Ever

So, for a week I stare at the clock in my classroom and wait for the big hand to touch a number and count by fives and try to remember if it was five after or five before the hour number.

"Phoebe!" Ms. Biz yells at me, "Why are you staring at the clock? Are you going somewhere? Did you finish the two rows of math problems you have to do?"

"Sorry, Ms. Biz, I just didn't want you to forget lunch," I answer her. "You know eating lunch is important for growing children." I couldn't say I was learning how to tell time because lots of kids in my class already know how.

"Phoebe, we already ate lunch. It's two o'clock in the afternoon and you've been staring at the clock all day," Ms. Biz says. "And, I want to see those math problems finished before you go home today because, if they're not finished, you will have a note to take home that says they must be completed for home-work tonight."

"Oh yeah, you're right, we did go to lunch, didn't we," I say. "But, Ms. Biz, we didn't go to gym yet, and exercise is important for growing children, too. I just want to make sure you don't forget and I don't mean to be rude, Ms. Biz, but I think it's five after two."

"Thank you, Phoebe, but please pay attention to this math lesson. We don't go to gym for twenty minutes," Ms. Biz reminds me.

Grandma Wig is coming over tonight and I

can't wait to show her how I can tell all the five minute times. Sometimes I get the befores and afters mixed up, but I am getting pretty good at it.

When I get home I give my mom the note that says I have to finish my math problems and take them back tomorrow.

"Phoebe, I am disappointed in you," Mom sighs. "Go up to your room and get that math done. Grandma is coming at six o'clock. You have two hours to finish it. Don't plan on going outside until it's done, either."

Yuck! I walk into my bedroom and throw my math book on my bed and watch it bounce up and down. Maybe, if I throw it hard enough, it'll bounce up and out the window. I look out the window and see Robbie playing football with some friends from school. He is so lucky. I grab my nerf football from under my bed and start to toss it up in the air. I can throw a pass so much better than Robbie can. I open my window. "Hey, Robbie! Look up here. Catch this!" I toss the football out the window and it sails right into Robbie's hands.

"Come on out, Phoebe. We need you!"

Robbie yells back.

"I will when I finish my math homework," I answer.

"You can do it down here. Watch this!" Robbie bends over and tosses the ball to one of his friends. "Twenty-four, thirty-six, forty-eight, hike!"

"Funny, Robbie," I answer. I sit down and try to do some math, but I hate it. I keep hearing Robbie and the guys playing football. Maybe I'll draw some pictures for Grandma Wig and then do my math.

Next thing I hear is the front door opening. Yea! Grandma Wig is here. I run down the stairs. "Hi, Grandma Wig, it's five minutes after six. You're five minutes late!"

"Phoebe Flower, you sweetie, Phoebe, you! You are the smartest little girl in the world. You learned all that in a week. I am so proud of you!" Grandma Wig laughs.

"I knew that in kindergarten," Amanda yells from the bedroom.

"Hi, Amanda!" Grandma Wig yells back. "You are smart, too. I know that."

"Amanda, come and help me with dinner

please," Mom calls. "Did you do your homework, Phoebe?"

"Just about," I tell her.

"Phoebe, will you sit down on the couch with me?" Grandma Wig asks me. "I have something to tell you."

I sit as close as I can to Grandma Wig.

"Phoebe, I have something for you. Your grandfather gave this to me many years ago. It's a very special treasure to me, but I want you to have it." Grandma Wig hands me a velvet box. I open up this velvet box and inside is the most beautiful watch I have ever seen. It's gold and shiny and it looks like something a movie star would wear.

"Grandma Wig!" I gasp, "Is this for me?"

"Yes, Phoebe, it is," Grandma Wig answers. "I thought to myself, 'How's Phoebe supposed to learn to tell time if she doesn't have a watch?' I even had your initials engraved on the back of it. See?"

I turn it over and there, on the back, is 'To P.F., with love.' It's the most beautiful thing I have ever seen. I think I will burst from happiness.

"Grandma Wig," I say, as I wrap my arms

hard around her neck, "this is the most special treasure anyone could ever have in their whole life. My heart is going to blow up. I'm so happy. Thank you!"

"You've already said thanks, Phoebe, by starting to learn how to tell time."

At dinner I can hardly eat anything. I can't stop staring at my new watch. Amanda smiles when I show it to her and says, 'Lovely," but when Grandma Wig leaves she says, "Big deal, Phoebe, you'll probably lose it in a week. You can't keep track of anything you own."

Before I take my bath to get ready for bed Mom warns, "Phoebe, did you finish all your homework? You don't have your watch on, do you?"

"Of course not, Mom," I answer, telling the truth for both questions. "I'm as careful with my watch as a mother robin is with her new babies."

When it's time for bed, I check to see if my watch is on my shelf, safe and sound, where I put it before my bath. The next morning all I can think about is showing my watch to Robbie and Elizabeth. I don't like Elizabeth very much and she doesn't like me. I can't wait to put on that watch, march onto that bus and ask Elizabeth if she wants to know what time it is.

Robbie's at the bus stop when I get there. "How come you're so early, Phoebe? You're usually running out the front door with a piece of toast in your mouth."

"Early? Is it early, Robbie? Let me check," I say as I roll up my sleeve. "Yes, you're right. It is early. My new watch that my grandmother gave me that is engraved with my initials P. F. on the back says the bus will be here in five minutes. Want to see it, Robbie?"

'Wow, Phoebe, your grandmother really gave that to you? That's a beauty! You're so lucky! Can you tell time?" Robbie asks me.

"Of course I can. I wouldn't wear a watch if I couldn't, silly," I tell him.

When the bus pulls up, I race up the stairs and jump into the seat next to Elizabeth. "Guess what time it is, Elizabeth?" I ask her.

"Who cares?" Elizabeth answers me.

"Everybody cares what time it is, Elizabeth. I have a watch my grandmother gave me with my initials P.F. engraved on the back. It's a very special treasure because it used to be hers. Want to see it?"

40

"Not really. I have a watch too. It has Mickey Mouse on it and I got mine at Disney World," Elizabeth brags.

"Are your initials on the back?" I grin.

"Big deal," Elizabeth says and turns her head to look out the window. I know she wishes she had a watch like mine.

# 7
# My Initials - Your Initials

When I get to school, I stop by Mrs. Ward's room to show her my new watch. "Your watch is so pretty, Phoebe. Be careful not to lose it. Your grandmother must love you very much to give you a watch like that."

"I'm as careful with this watch as a mother robin is with her baby birds," I tell Mrs. Ward.

"It's a very special treasure, you know."

Ms. Biz lets me show my watch for "show and tell." I tell the class that my initials, P.F., are engraved on the back. "How can your initials be P.F. if both Phoebe and Flower start with the 'F' sound, Phoebe?" Gloria asks.

"Good question, Gloria," Ms. Biz answers. "When a P and an H are together they make the 'F' sound. Phoebe starts that way and so do phone and Philip. This is a good learning experience for us, Phoebe. Thank you!"

I smile.

Then Ms. Biz gives me a message to take to the office because she knows I want to show my watch to Mrs. Walkerspeaking. "Hey, Mrs. Walkerspeaking, do you know what time it is?

"No, Phoebe, what time is it?" she asks me.

"It's five minutes to ten o'clock. What do you think of that?" I ask her.

"That is a very good time, Phoebe. Thanks!" Mrs. Walkerspeaking answers.

All day long I have to remind Ms. Biz what time it is. She says, "Thank you very much, Phoebe, but could you do some school work? I want to see your homework on my desk from yesterday before you go home today." I am too excited to do school work, so I look at my watch and practice telling time.

When we go to music, Miss Prissy Fasola asks me, "Phoebe, why are you looking at your wrist today and not singing? Last week, I asked you not to sing so loudly. I didn't mean for you to not sing at all."

"Don't you know, Miss Prissy Fasola," Elizabeth yells out, "Phoebe has a very special treasure. The whole wide world knows Phoebe got a new watch."

"Yes, I did," I answer, proudly, "and it has my initials, P.F., right on the back. The same initials that you have, Miss Prissy Fasola. Want me to show you my initials?"

"Don't take it off, Phoebe. You'll lose it," she tells me. "I believe you."

All day long I tell everyone I see what time it is. I love my new watch. I don't even mind being in school. I know when it's time to go home without anyone telling me. I can't wait to write my dad and tell him about my new watch. He'll be so happy and proud of me.

I jump on the school bus, "Hi, Mike!" I greet the bus driver, "Do you know that it is almost ten minutes after three? You are right on time today. Good job!"

"Thanks, Phoebe," Mike smiles.

"Almost ten after three?" Elizabeth asks, as I sit down, "Don't you know exactly what time that is? What good is a new watch if you can't read it?"

"Of course, I know, Elizabeth. I just didn't want to make Mike nervous and think he was late," I answer, thinking that I better call Grandma Wig and ask her how to tell time EXACTLY.

When Robbie and I get off the bus, I see the mail truck coming down the street. I decide to wait and tell Bill, the mailman, that he is right on time today. I just love this watch. I roll up my sleeve and giggle when I see this beautiful gold watch that is mine, all mine.

"Hi Bill!" I yell, "I just want you to know you're right on time today. It's three thirty! You're doing a great job!"

"Hey, Phoebe, look up!" Robbie calls from his front yard, "catch this!"

I turn around and see a football heading straight toward my head. I duck fast. The football zooms past me, through the mail truck

window and into Bill's bag of mail.

"So sorry, Bill, I'll get it." I run over to the truck, reach my hands into the mailbag moving letters and magazines and pull out the ball.

"I guess Robbie needs to practice his passing, doesn't he?" Bill grins.

"Maybe he thought he was playing basketball," I laugh.

"Bye, Phoebe, stay out of trouble," Bill yells as I skip-hop into my house.

"Listen carefully, girls. We have to eat dinner early because I have to stop at the drugstore before we go to Amanda's dance lessons. So, do your homework and then help set the table. Can one of you play with Walter while I cook dinner?"

"I'll play with Walter," I volunteer.

"Phoebe, first, I have to talk to you," Mom says in an angry voice. "Ms. Biz called me today and said that you did not have your homework done today. I am putting my foot down once and for all. If you don't get your work done in school you will not be allowed out of this house for one whole week unless it's to go to school. Do you understand that? I really mean business, Phoebe. Now go upstairs and get your homework done so we can eat and go to dance lessons. Amanda will play with Walter."

This time I can tell Mom really means it. I go upstairs and lock myself in the bathroom to do my homework. I only have six more problems to go when my mother calls, "Phoebe Flower, time to eat!"

The rest of the night is crazy! We get a flat tire on the way home from dance lessons. Mom reads us our bedtime story while we are in the bathtub. Amanda can't find one of her red shoes that she insists on wearing to school tomorrow, so we all have to hunt for that.

# 8

# Lost, But Not Found

All night long I dream about bars on my window and guards standing at the front and back door of my house so I can't sneak out. When I wake up the next morning, I'm thinking about how I can finish those six problems before it's time for math. Maybe Robbie can help me.

"Hey, Robbie!" I yell as I cross the street to wait for the school bus. "I need your help! You've got to save me."

"Let me guess, Phoebe. You lost your watch," Robbie says.

I freeze! I reach for my wrist and feel my whole body getting hot. My legs start to shake. There is no watch. The watch is not on my wrist. I grab the other wrist. It's not there, either. I start shaking and screaming, "ROBBIE, HELP!! My watch is gone. Where do you think it is?"

"Gee, Phoebe, I don't know, but you better get out of the road. You're going to get hit by a car."

"Hit by a car? Is that all you can think of? My watch is gone, my watch that is a very special treasure and has my initials on the back that my grandmother gave me that my grandfather gave her. I have to find my watch." I sob and move out of the road.

"Here comes the bus, Phoebe. Just think about where you wore it last," Robbie says trying to help me. "We'll find it!"

I drag my feet up the stairs of the school bus

thinking about what Robbie said. Where did I wear it last? That is the big question. I can't think. My brain isn't working. All I can think about is my Grandma's sad face when she finds out I lost that watch. Everybody thought I'd lose it and now I did. There is no way I can let anybody know I lost it.

"Don't sit next to me, Phoebe, if you're going to tell me what time it is every second," Elizabeth warns me.

I don't say a word. I walk past Elizabeth and find a seat by myself. I have to think. I have to think hard. I remember! I showed it for "show and tell." I jump out of my seat as soon as the bus slows down. "Phoebe Flower," the bus driver yells, "stay in your seat until the bus stops!"

I walk the fast walk down the hall to my classroom. Ms. Biz is writing on the chalkboard. "Hi, Phoebe, you're the first one here today. You're usually last. Did you run?"

"Oh no, Ms. Biz, I walked the fast walk. Can I ask you something?"

"Sure, Phoebe, what is it?" Ms. Biz asks me.

"Did you find anything yesterday in the

classroom that shouldn't be here after all the kids left to go home?"

"I don't understand what you're asking. What should I have found?"

"Well, you know, if somebody lost something and they couldn't find it and then you saw something that you thought shouldn't be just laying around in a classroom after all the kids were gone . . ." I tried to explain.

I begin to hear the rest of the kids coming in the door.

"Did you lose something, Phoebe?" Ms. Biz asks.

"I'm not really sure if I did or didn't, but if I did, please, Ms. Biz, did you find it?" I take a deep breath and close my eyes.

"Oh, I understand, Phoebe. No, I'm sorry I didn't, but, if you want to check Lost and Found, why don't you go to the office? Good luck!" Ms. Biz gives me a hug.

"Good idea," I think, and hurry off to ask Mrs. Walkerspeaking.

It's kind of busy in the office, but I wiggle through all the adults. I say, "Excuse me, excuse me, this is an emergency." Everyone probably thinks I'm going to throw up so they move aside. I finally get to Mrs. Walkerspeaking's desk and tap her on the shoulder.

"Mrs. Walkerspeaking, I need your help. Is anything in the Lost and Found box that shouldn't be there?" I ask, huffing and puffing from squeezing through the crowd.

"Yes, Phoebe, everything in the Lost and Found box shouldn't be there," she giggles.

"That was funny, Mrs. Walkerspeaking, but this is sort of an emergency. Someone has lost something that is very special and it shouldn't be lost. Can I look in the Lost and Found box, please?"

"Sure, Phoebe, but I don't think what you're looking for is there. No one has turned in anything in two days except an old chewed up pencil and I doubt you're looking for that. Oh no!" Mrs. Walkerspeaking gasps, "You didn't lose the watch your grandmother gave you?"

Tears start to fill my eyes.

"Have you asked Ms. Biz? Did you check with Mr. Gordon, the custodian? Did you have Art, Music or Gym yesterday? Did you ask the bus driver?" Mrs. Walkerspeaking asks,

almost out of breath.

"Yes, no, yes, music, and no." I try to answer all at once.

"Well, Phoebe, first, I'd ask Mr. Gordon, and then, I'd ask your bus driver. You'll have to wait to ask Miss Prissy Fasola. She called in sick with the flu, and I don't think she'll be back for a few days. Good luck, Phoebe, and don't worry, you'll find it." Mrs. Walkerspeaking squeezes my hand.

I leave the office and go to find Mr. Gordon. As I walk past the broom closet, I hear, "Pssst!" Robbie's sticks his head out the door and holds up his magnifying glass to show me. "Don't look in here, Phoebe," Robbie whispers, "I've already searched it out and there is no evidence of a watch. Don't worry, Phoebe, we'll find it."

Robbie always makes me smile.

I find Mr. Gordon and he says he hasn't seen anything gold and shiny with initials on the back, but he'd let me know if he did. The rest of the day I do nothing but think about where that beautiful watch could be. Ms. Biz must feel sorry for me because she doesn't call on me at all. She doesn't even ask if I have my homework finished. When it is time to go home, I try to be the first one on the bus so I can ask Mike if he found it. "Nothing was turned in, Phoebe," Mike tells me, "but I will check all the seats carefully when the kids get off the bus."

"You're the best, Mike!" I tell him.

# 9

# Vacuum Disaster

Robbie gets on the bus and sits next to me. "Hey, Phoebe, any luck finding you-know-what?"

"None!" I answer. I tell him where I looked.

"Want me to come over to your house and help you search? I don't have much homework. If you're really feeling brave, we could always go to Miss Prissy Fasola's house and then you wouldn't have to wait two days to ask her," Robbie says.

"Wow, you are a good friend, Robbie. I don't even like to talk to Miss Prissy when she feels good. Think about what a grouch she must be when she has the flu. It's a scary thought." We both laugh. "Thanks for offering to help, but I don't want anyone in my family to even guess I lost the watch. Amanda might think it's weird if we're both looking under tables and chairs.

When I get home, I try to act normal so no one will notice me. "Hello, Mother, hello, Walter," I say. I hang up my coat and put away my book bag and have a snack. Amanda is still at cheerleading practice, so this is a great time to look for my watch.

"Phoebe, what's wrong with you?" my mother asks.

"Wrong? Why do you say wrong?" I answer my mother.

"Well, for one thing you hung up your coat and put away your book bag, which you never do, and the next thing is you walked right past the brand new vacuum I bought today and you didn't notice it. Remember my old one?

It wouldn't pick up air. This one works perfectly.
I vacuumed all day. I vacuumed the whole
house. This new vacuum is so strong, I think it
could vacuum up our car," Mom laughs. I want
to cry.

I go to my room, close the door, and put the
pillow over my head. There is no use looking.
I'm sure my mother vacuumed it up. I tell Mom
I'm sick and can't come down to dinner.

When I wake up, Mom is feeling my fore-
head. "Phoebe, are you OK? It's morning and
you slept through the night. Is something

bothering you?"

"No, everything's fine. It's just . . . ah . . . " I start to tell her.

"Did you ever find my red shoe?" Amanda asks as she opens my door.

"It's late, Mom," I say as I jump out of bed, "I better get ready for school."

Today is worse than yesterday. I have no more ideas where to look for that beautiful, shiny special watch. Ms. Biz doesn't feel sorry for me anymore. She calls on me twice. At least she doesn't send home another note. Robbie tries to cheer me up by telling me jokes. I pretend to laugh so he feels better. When I get home from school, I am sadder than I was when I left. How will I ever go to school tomorrow?

Mom is waiting for me when I come in the house, "Great news, Phoebe. I've got something to cheer you up. Guess who's coming for dinner?"

Mom doesn't realize the only thing that would cheer me up is if our new vacuum got the flu and threw up my watch.

"Who?" I ask.

"Your favorite person in the whole world."

"Grandma Wig!" I scream. "No, not tonight, Mom. You must be joking!"

"Phoebe Flower, you love Grandma Wig. What is wrong with you?" Mom looks shocked.

"She can't come tonight, Mom. I think I'm getting sick. You don't want her to catch it, do you?"

"Phoebe, you are not getting sick and Grandma Wig is coming, so you better change your attitude very quickly. Now go upstairs and do your homework so you can visit with her," Mom says angrily.

I go upstairs to do my homework. Amanda pops open her door and says with a smile, "I agree with you this time, Phoebe. I think you are sick . . . sick in the head."

I run to my bedroom and slam the door. How will I ever keep Grandma Wig from asking me what time it is? Once Amanda discovers I don't want to talk about it, she'll find out I lost the watch.

I hear the phone ringing. Maybe Grandma Wig is calling to say she can't come.

# 10
## Now That's a Great Idea!

"PHOEBE!" My mom is calling my name.
I open my bedroom door.

"The telephone is for you, Phoebe," Mom
yells.

It's probably Robbie with another joke.
"Hello!" I say.

"Hello, is this Phoebe Flower?" the voice
asks.

"Yep, who is this?" I answer.

"Well, Phoebe, this is Miss Prissy Fasola and I think I have something that belongs to you."

"**Who** did you say this is?" I ask.

" I said . . . this is Miss Prissy FASOLA! Do you want me to sing it to you? I went to my mailbox today and found an envelope from Bill, the mailman. I will read you the note that was inside.

Dear Miss Fasola,

Yesterday, I found a woman's watch in the bottom of my mailbag. I have no idea how it got there, but it has your initials on it, so I decided it must be yours.

> Sincerely,
> Bill

Well, Phoebe, it is not my watch and I remember two days ago you were telling everyone in the school the time, and I thought it just might be yours."

"Miss Fasola, it **is** my watch! Do you really have my very special treasure? Can I come to your house right now and get it, please? You are so wonderful, Miss Prissy Fasola. Just now

I was thinking my life was over. You have saved my grandmother from being sad. You have saved my life. Thank you, thank you, thank you."

I slam down the phone without waiting for Miss Fasola to answer me. I run down the stairs and out the front door and yell to my mother that I will be right back.

"Where are you going?" my mother calls as I run as fast as I can to Robbie's house. I knock and Robbie comes to the front door. I grab his arm and pull him down the street by his shirtsleeve. "Where are we going?" he yells.

"To Miss Fasola's house." I try to sound calm.

"You must be kidding, Phoebe. You're just one big kidder. Tell me you're kidding. There is no way you'd go there," Robbie pants as we run.

"She's got my watch, Robbie. We have to." I start to get a funny feeling in my stomach as we get closer to Miss Fasola's house. I've never been to a teacher's house before.

I run up the porch stairs and ring the doorbell twice. Robbie hides underneath the front porch.

The door opens—"Ah, ah, ah, Miss Prissy Fasola," I pant out of breath, "I'm Phoebe Flower. We have the same initials."

"I know who you are, Phoebe, I called you, remember?" Miss Fasola was dressed in a long pink bathrobe. She looked sick.

"Come in Phoebe. You, too, Robbie. You must be uncomfortable under the porch. I'll go get your watch. It's upstairs in my jewelry box where a watch should be when it's not being worn." Miss Fasola's phone rings. "Come inside, both of you. I won't bite. Wait here. I have to answer the phone, first."

Robbie and I look at each other. Robbie is shaking. We step inside to wait. Hurry up, Miss Fasola, I think to myself. Don't take too long. We could hear her talking on the upstairs phone. Did she forget we were waiting?

Then I see it! In the corner of the living room is a very big, no, an enormous, black, shiny piano—bigger than even a car. I nudge Robbie and point to it. He just stands there, not moving an inch. "Maybe," I whisper to him, "I'll just tip-toe run over to that shiny piano so I can take a closer look. I've never seen

anything so big."

Robbie's eyes open like saucers. "Are you a complete nut?  Do you want to die?  Stay right here, Phoebe."

I look up the stairs. I don't hear Miss Fasola coming.  I tiptoe run over to the piano as quietly as I can. Those white piano keys are smiling at me like shiny white teeth.  I have to touch them.  They feel so cool and smooth.

"PHOEBE  FLOWER,  WHAT  ARE DOING?" I feel two hands pressing on my shoulders.

"Oh, I'm so sorry, Miss Fasola. I didn't mean to touch it.  I just couldn't help it."

"Don't be sorry, Phoebe.  I mean, what are you doing playing the piano?  Who taught you to play?  Do you know you are playing 'Mary Had A Little Lamb'? Do you take piano lessons?"

"No, I just figured it out.  Doesn't everybody know how to do that?" I say.

"No, everybody doesn't know how. Come on over and listen to Phoebe play, Robbie.  I think I have a wonderful idea!"

Miss Fasola tells us her idea.

We skip-run all the way back. When we get to Robbie's house, we slap each other a high-five. It's been a wonderful day—the best day ever! "You are the greatest friend in the whole world. Thanks for helping me find my lost treasure, Robbie!" I tell him as I look at my watch.

I run to my house and burst open my front door.

"Where have you been?" Mom calls to me from the kitchen, "We've been worried about you."

"Grandma Wig, Mom, Amanda, Walter, Buddy Dog, do you want to know what time it is?" I shout.

"Sure, Phoebe! What time is it?" Grandma Wig answers.

"It's time for me to be determined to play a **piano** solo all by myself in the second grade concert at the end of the year. Miss Prissy Fasola says if I practice long enough and hard enough I will see the whole audience stand and clap and cheer."

Grandma Wig walks over to me, puts her arms around me. I close my eyes. I feel so good.